For Maria Modugno
—C.G.

To Santi and Tian
—L.E.

Text copyright © 2023 by Chris Grabenstein
Jacket art and interior illustrations copyright © 2023 by Leo Espinosa

Visit us on the Web! rhcbooks.com

Educators and librarians, for a variety of teaching tools, visit us at RHTeachersLibrarians.com

Library of Congress Cataloging-in-Publication Data
Names: Grabenstein, Chris, author. | Espinosa, Leo, illustrator.
Title: NO is all i know / Chris Grabenstein; pictures by Leo Espinosa. Description: First edition. |
New York: Random House Children's Books, [2023] | Audience: Ages 3–7. |
Summary: "Toddler Oliver says 'no' to everything—from brushing his teeth and cleaning to swinging on the swings—
until his cousin Jess comes to visit and Oliver discovers all that is possible when you say 'yes.'"—Provided by publisher.
Identifiers: LCCN 2021043965 | ISBN 978-0-593-30204-0 (hardcover) | ISBN 978-0-593-30205-7 (library binding) |
ISBN 978-0-593-30206-4 (ebook)
Subjects: CYAC: Behavior—Fiction. | Change—Fiction. | LCGFT: Picture Books.
Classification: LCC PZ7.G7487 No 2023 | DDC [E]—dc23

The text of this book is set in 16-point Archer Medium.
The illustrations were created with a mighty pencil and Adobe Photoshop.
Book design by Nicole de las Heras

MANUFACTURED IN CHINA
10 9 8 7 6 5 4 3 2 1
First Edition

NO
Is All I Know!

written by
Chris Grabenstein

pictures by
Leo Espinosa

Random House New York

Oliver McSnow would always say

no!

no matter what you asked him.

Did he brush his teeth?

NO!

Was he hungry?

NO!

Would he clean up his mess?

NO!

Did he want to swing on the swings?

NNNNOOOOO!

Oliver said NO! so many times . . .

. . . his NO! started to grow.

"Oliver, please put away your toys!" said his mom.

His NO! became so strong . . .

. . . there was no way to stop it.

"Are you ready to get dressed?" asked his mom.

Would he like to play with his cousin Jess?

He even said NO! to ice cream!

And puzzles and painting and pizza and pudding and Popsicles.

Before long, Oliver McSnow had the world's strongest NO!

He said NO! to all kinds of food.

So all he ever ate was macaroni and cheese.

Morning, noon, and night.

Breakfast, lunch, and dinner.

He never took a bath.

(Even though all that mac and cheese
made him smell cheesy.)

He wouldn't fall asleep when he went to bed.
(Because NO! was all he ever said.)

But one morning . . .

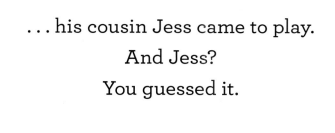

. . . his cousin Jess came to play.

And Jess?

You guessed it.

Jess liked to say YES!

"Would you kids like to go outside?" asked Oliver's father.

Oliver was too tired and too full of macaroni and cheese
to say NO! before Jess said YES!
And so, outside they went . . .

. . . where Jess said YES! to everything!

Suddenly—thanks to Jess and his super-powerful YES!—
Oliver's world was full of new things.
New food.
New fun.
New friends.

Later, they played with toys that could become whatever they yessed them to be.

"This duck is a submarine!"

"Yes! And its koala bear captain juggles ice cream underwater!"

"What a great day we had today!" said Jess with a yawn.
"Tomorrow will you go back to saying NO?"

Oliver thought.

Then he thought again.
And do you know what he said?